CHARLIE·PIECHART

and the case of the

Missing Hat

Hey, kids! Haberdashery and rocket construction can be tricky when you're using tools like scissors and staplers, so before you become a princess or shoot off into space, make sure you have an adult nearby, okay?

For my art teachers, Brent Lowman, Rudy Kovaks,
Jon Anderson, and Glen Edwards—E.C.

For Cheryl Steris, a passionate and talented
former teacher and principal who kindly
helped me navigate geometry—M.S.

Katherine Tegen Books is an imprint of HarperCollins Publishers.

Charlie Piechart and the Case of the Missing Hat
Text copyright © 2016 by Marilyn Sadler and Eric Comstock
Illustrations copyright © 2016 by Eric Comstock
All rights reserved. Manufactured in China.
No part of this book may be used or reproduced in any manner whatsoever without written permission except in the case of
brief quotations embodied in critical articles and reviews. For information address HarperCollins Children's Books, a division
of HarperCollins Publishers, 195 Broadway, New York, NY 10007. www.harpercollinschildrens.com

Library of Congress Control Number: 2015952457
ISBN 978-0-06-237056-3

The artist used pencil, paper, Adobe Illustrator, and Adobe Photoshop to create the digital illustrations for this book.
Typography by Eric Comstock and Dana Fritts
16 17 18 19 20 SCP 10 9 8 7 6 5 4 3 2 1
❖
First Edition

CHARLIE·PIECHART
and the case of the
Missing Hat

written by **ERIC COMSTOCK** & **MARILYN SADLER**   illustrated by **ERIC COMSTOCK**

a
CHARLIE
PIECHART
mystery

KT KATHERINE TEGEN BOOKS
An Imprint of HarperCollins Publishers

The school bell had rung, and Charlie and Watson were on their way to math club.

It was Charlie's friend Margot.
"I'm Princess Violet in the school play tonight,"
Margot said, "but my princess hat is missing!"

Margot drew a picture of her hat.

Can you find it for me, Charlie?

"I painted it purple in art class today," she explained, "then I put sparkly sparkles all over it."

Charlie noticed it was shaped like a cone.

Charlie and Watson started
their search in the art room.

They looked and looked for a **cone-shaped** hat.

Watson found so many
different shapes.

"That hat is **sphere**-shaped,"
said Charlie.

(Moonwalk)

←

Sphere

"That hat is shaped
like a **cylinder**."

Cylinder

"That's a **cone**, Watson, but it's not Margot's princess hat."

Cone

"I don't know what shape that is, but it sure looks like Principal George's hat!"

Watson, your paws are purple!

Watson's paw prints led Charlie to a table with a purple circle on it.

Charlie and Watson spotted a trail of purple sparkles.

The paint is still wet, and there are sparkles stuck to it!

DID YOU KNOW? The bottom of a cone is a circle! →

They followed it out of the art room and into the hallway.

"STOP, Janitor Bob! Our evidence!"

But it was too late. Janitor Bob had vacuumed up part of the trail.

"These sparkles are all over the school!" said Janitor Bob. "I saw some in the teachers' lounge, more in the auditorium, and lots in the science lab."

Now Charlie had three new clues. Plus, he had never been to the teachers' lounge before.

Sparkle Sightings

☑ Art Room

Science Lab

HALF MONTH | TOTAL $
OUT | IN | OUT | IN | OUT

Auditorium

Teachers' Lounge

So Charlie and Watson followed the sparkles to the teachers' lounge.

TEACHERS'
LOUNGE

But the trail didn't lead to a purple hat. It led to a sparkly cake.

Did you know?

A birthday cake,

a shoe box,

and a cereal box are all **rectangular prisms!**

Next on Charlie's list was the auditorium.

Charlie asked his friend Henry if he had seen Margot's hat. But Henry was too busy practicing his lines for the play.

RIBBIT!

RIBBIT!

RIBBIT!

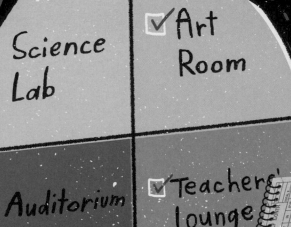

Science Lab

☑ Art Room

Auditorium

☑ Teachers' Lounge

Charlie's sister Kate hadn't seen Margot's hat, either.

Ask the mushrooms, Charlie. Maybe they've seen it.

The mushrooms?

"Nope," said the mushrooms. "Our hats are polka-dotted half **spheres**, and our stems are striped **cylinders**."

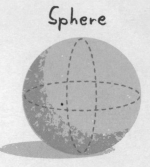

Half Sphere   Sphere

Charlie spotted a ring of purple paint and sparkles on the table in the science lab. Then he noticed the board was filled with drawings of rockets and space travel.

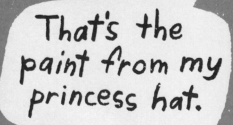

That's the paint from my princess hat.

But it was too late!

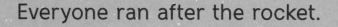

Everyone ran after the rocket.

Then they watched as the
rocket fell softly to earth. . . .

"The tip of the rocket is landing on Margot's head!" said Charlie.

Look at that!

HOW TO MAKE A
PRINCESS HAT

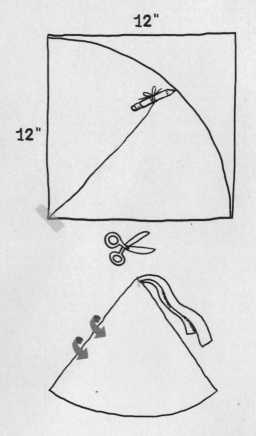

1. Start with a square sheet of poster board that is 12"x12".

2. Tape a string to one corner and tie a pencil to the other end of the string.

3. Pull the string tight and draw a quarter circle.

4. Cut along the line with scissors.

5. Every princess hat needs streamers. Use crepe paper. Tape the crepe paper to the tip of your quarter circle.

6. Roll your quarter circle into a cone shape. Staple the seam at the base. Use masking tape to cover the rest of the seam.

7. Paint your hat and add glitter.

HOW TO MAKE A
ROCKET

* To make the rocket cone, follow steps 1-6 from the princess hat instructions.

7. Make a cylinder by rolling a 12"x18" poster board into a tube. Staple each end of the cylinder and add masking tape.

8. Cut an 8" circle from a poster board. Cut the circle into 4 quarters.

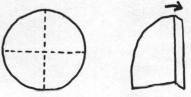

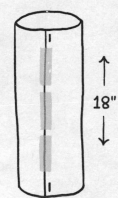

18"

9. Fold each quarter circle and tape to the cylinder as shown.

10. Paint the rocket. Pretend to fly your rocket while you make rocket noises.

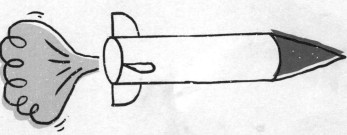

SHAPES *ARE* EVERYWHERE!

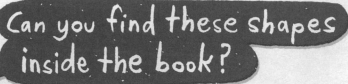
Can you find these shapes inside the book?

. . . in my locker
Can you find **3 rectangular prisms**?

. . . in the art room
Can you find a face shaped like a **cube**?

. . . on the school bulletin board
Can you find a **hexagon**?

. . . on my sister Kate
Can you find a costume shaped like a **sphere**?

. . . in Margot's hair
Can you find a hair clip shaped like **2 triangles**?

. . . in the princess tower
Can you find a brick shaped like a **rectangle?**

. . . in the sky
Can you find a cloud shaped like
Principal George's hat?

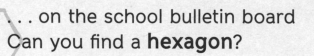